*To the contrary heroes:*
*May your gardens grow. —C.B.*

*To all the magical gardens I played in as a child*
*in my birth country, Kosova—thank you for the*
*inspiration. —A.L.*

# The Secret Garden

adapted by Calista Brill

based on the novel by Frances Hodgson Burnett

illustrated by Adelina Lirius

**HARPER**

*An Imprint of HarperCollinsPublishers*

# Once upon a time . . .

a walled garden bloomed under the summer skies
in the north of England.

But it was locked up and left all alone.

And it stayed all alone, for many years.

Until . . .

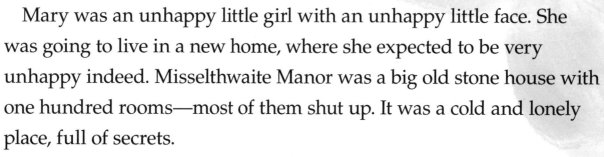

Mary was an unhappy little girl with an unhappy little face. She was going to live in a new home, where she expected to be very unhappy indeed. Misselthwaite Manor was a big old stone house with one hundred rooms—most of them shut up. It was a cold and lonely place, full of secrets.

Mary arrived on a winter night, when the wind was howling across the moor and rain was pouring down.

In the morning, Mary woke up alone.
The house was silent around her.

At first, Mary hated Misselthwaite Manor. She hated
the cold, echoing hallways. She hated the barren, scrubby
moor. She even hated the nice, hot breakfast that Martha,
the maid, brought to her room.

One morning, Mary took her skipping rope and went out to explore.
The house had many gardens, but they were mostly brown and bare
in winter.

Soon she met an old gardener named Ben.

"I'll tell you a secret," he said. Mary listened eagerly, and Ben told
her about a hidden garden at Misselthwaite Manor, tucked away
somewhere in the walls and hedges, locked up tight.

Mary liked having a secret.

Skip, skip, skip went Mary around the gardens. Skip, skip—oh!

"Hello," said Mary to the robin. His cheerful red breast was the only color she could see on that cold, gray day.

"He's made up his mind to be friends with you," said Ben.

Mary liked having a friend.

Before long, Mary found she even liked the cold, wet air that blew in off the moor in the late winter. Day by day, Mary's thin, pale face got rounder and pinker. For the first time in her life, she was hungry in the morning and sleepy at bedtime.

One day the rain was too heavy for Mary to play outside.
So she decided to explore the big, old, sad house.

Up hallways and down stairs she went, turning corner
after corner, wandering in and out of dusty rooms. She
never saw anyone.

But she heard someone—someone crying.

"Who was it?" Mary asked Martha that night.

"Just your imagination," Martha replied.

The days grew longer and brighter as winter started to fade. Mary found that she could now skip all the way around the gardens without stopping even once.

"Ninety-eight! Ninety-nine! One hundred!" Mary counted as she skipped. She rested by a wall covered in ivy and she thought about the secret garden, locked up and left all alone.

"Chirp!" cried the robin, pecking at the dirt.
Something gleamed and glittered. . . .
    A key!

The garden had been alone for a long time. Brown, scratchy
rosebushes climbed the trees and trailed from branch to branch.
Years of fallen leaves covered the ground like a gray blanket.
Was the garden dead? Or just sleeping?

*Something* was alive—something was struggling to reach the light and greet the spring.

Mary took a deep breath and thought very hard. She loved the garden already, and, more than anything, she wanted it to stay a secret. But she needed help.

"I need some advice," Mary told Martha. "About . . . a little garden." She did not say which one.

"You'll be wanting Dickon," Martha said. Her brother knew everything about plants and animals.

So Martha sent for him. And the moment Mary met Dickon, she knew she could trust him with any secret.

With Dickon's help, Mary learned how to care for the garden.
And as the spring came on, the garden burst to life.

Misselthwaite Manor had one other secret. His name was Colin, and he was sick, sad, angry, and weak.

It was Colin who had been crying that day. And it was Colin's crying that reached Mary's ears and brought her to him one stormy spring night.

"Are you a ghost?" he asked her.
"Are you?" Mary said.

Colin's father was the master of Misselthwaite Manor. But he was never home. Colin couldn't walk, and he hated it when people felt sorry for him. So he hid in his room and never went out.

"*I* don't feel sorry for you," Mary told Colin. She thought he was a bit like the garden—he'd been locked up and left alone for too long.

Dickon had known how to help the garden. Maybe he would know how to help Colin, too. So Mary brought Dickon to visit, and Dickon brought his animals.

"What you need," Dickon told Colin, "is some fresh spring air."

The robin had been Mary's first friend, but now she had two others.
Mary, Dickon, and Colin worked in the secret garden every day.
And every day more flowers appeared. Delphiniums, foxgloves, and
irises lined the walks.

"It's like Magic," Mary said. She felt a little foolish saying it out loud. But Dickon nodded, and so did Colin.

"It *is* Magic," said Colin.

Day by day, the Magic of the garden—and the spring air and the birdsong and the work of digging and watering—made Colin strong and cheerful. It made Mary happy, just looking at him.

And on the day that the roses finally burst into bloom . . .

Colin walked.

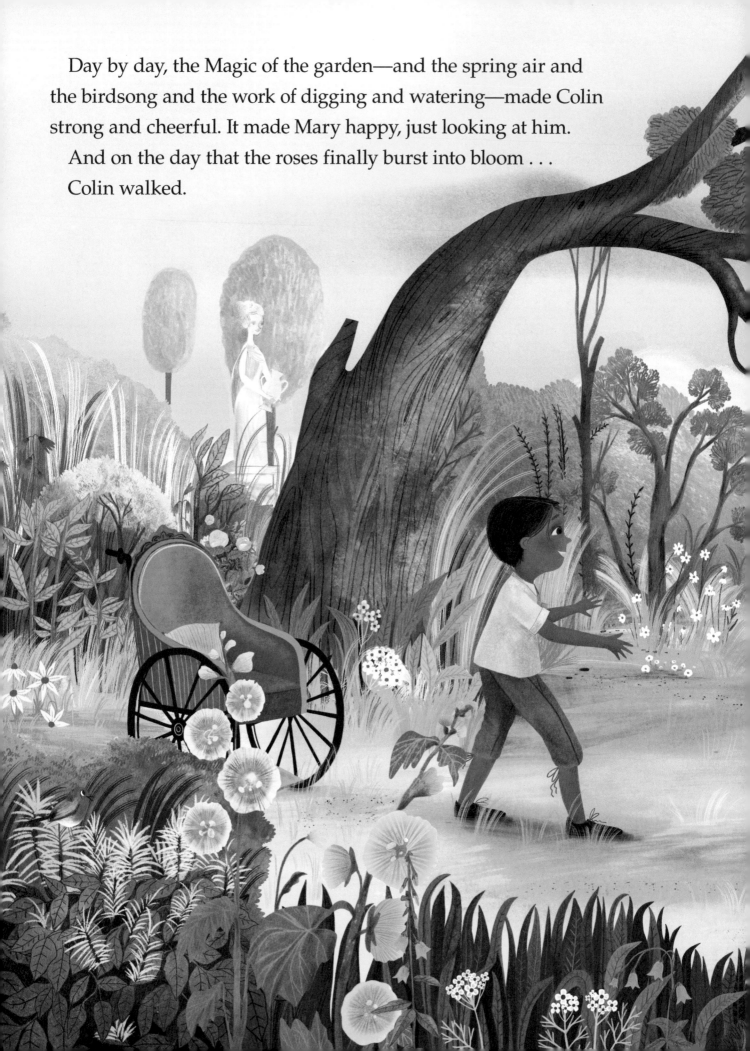

The End

## About The Secret Garden

Written by Frances Hodgson Burnett over a century ago, *The Secret Garden* is one of the most beloved children's novels of all time. Generations of readers have lost themselves in its descriptions of the hopeful spring emerging from the gloomy Yorkshire winter and the heartwarming friendship that develops among Mary, Dickon, and Colin. The story has been retold in many forms: on the stage, in the movies, on television, and, yes, in picture books like this one.

Mary Lennox is an unusual heroine because she is decidedly not lovable when we first meet her. She's plain, selfish, crabby, and uninterested in other people. But she is without a doubt the hero of our story from the very first page, despite all her many unlikable qualities. For me, that's what makes *The Secret Garden* so important: It presents us with an unloved and unlovable little girl and asks us not to love her (at least not right away) but to do something harder and arguably more important—to believe in her. To have faith that she will find her way. That she, like her garden, will grow into something splendid.

—C.B.